# TWISTED
## FAIRY TALES

# Little **Rude** Riding Hood

## JO FRANKLIN

### ARCTURUS

ARCTURUS

This edition published in 2020 by Arcturus Publishing Limited
26/27 Bickels Yard, 151–153 Bermondsey Street,
London SE1 3HA

Written by Jo Franklin
Illustrated by Chris Jevons
Designed by Jeni Child
Edited by Sebastian Rydberg and Samantha Newman

ISBN: 978-1-78950-246-6
CH006829NT
Supplier 13, Date 1119, Print run 9054

Printed in China

There was once a girl who lived in a tiny little house, in a tiny little village on the edge of a great big forest. She lived with her lovely mother and father, who ran the village bakery. Father served the customers while Mother baked fresh bread and delicious cakes to sell in the store.

The family had a snug home, plenty to eat, and would have been very happy, except for just one thing ...

The little girl hadn't learned good manners. She always did whatever she wanted, and it was usually very rude!

When Father let her choose a cake to eat from the bakery, she pushed past all the

customers and grabbed the biggest cake for herself.

"That's very rude," Father said.

The girl grinned at him, with her mouth full of cake. "I don't care," she said, spitting crumbs everywhere.

On her birthday, the mailman arrived with a present from her Grandma.

The little girl snatched the parcel out of his hands and ripped it open. Inside was a bright red, super-soft coat with a hood.

The little girl liked the coat a lot and put it on straight away.

"You must write to your Grandma and say thank you," said Mother.

"Boring! I shan't," the girl said, poking out her tongue.

"How rude!" the mailman said as he cycled away.

From that day on, she was known as Little Rude Riding Hood.

Mother and Father worried that Little
Rude Riding Hood had upset her Grandma
by not thanking her for the beautiful coat she
had sent.

So, one day, Mother filled a basket with
special cakes and took them to Little Rude.

"It's Grandma's birthday today, so Father
and I thought you could take these cakes to
her, as a present from us all," Mother said.

Little Rude rolled her eyes, "How can Grandma be having another birthday? She's already so old!"

"Please will you take them? Father and I have to work, and your Grandma is excited to see you," said Mother. "Besides, you still need to thank her for your birthday present."

Little Rude sighed, "Fine."

"Thank you," said Mother. "Remember, if you meet anyone on the way, be very polite to them. Say 'Please,' 'Thank you,' and all the other magic words."

Little Rude took the basket and set off to walk to Grandma's house. It was a long way away, through the woods.

Little Rude made up rude songs as she walked. Then, when she got bored of that, she started trying to blow the biggest raspberry she could. She was blowing so hard that she wasn't looking where she was going, and she bumped straight into a wolf who was waiting at a crossroads! He tumbled to the ground.

"Hey!" said Mr. Wolf, angrily. "Look where you're going!"

"Why should I?" said Little Rude.

Mr. Wolf had been going to special classes to help him manage his temper. He took a deep breath, and counted to ten. "It's just not polite," he said, "to knock people over."

Little Rude stared at him for a minute, then she laughed.

Mr. Wolf was startled. "Why are you laughing?" he asked.

"Because you just got knocked over by a little girl," Little Rude chuckled. "I've seen lambs who are stronger than you!"

"How rude!" said Mr. Wolf. No one had ever dared speak to him like that before.

Little Rude swished her hood up and walked on through the forest.

Little Rude had never walked to Grandma's on her own before, and she wasn't very sure of the way. She took a few wrong turns and, though she didn't realize it, she ended up back at the crossroads with Mr. Wolf.

Little Rude put her nose in the air. "Urgh, this wolf is even stinkier than the one I passed before!" she said loudly.

Although she was being rude, Mr. Wolf tried very hard to be polite. "You must be lost. Where are you trying to go?" he asked.

"I'm going to Grandma's house," said Little Rude.

"I know where your grandma lives. I can help you find the way," said Mr. Wolf.

"Perhaps you should find your way to a dentist, to see to your silly big teeth!" laughed Little Rude.

Mr. Wolf was very upset. "Fine," growled Mr. Wolf, "I won't help you then."

"Good," Little Rude folded her arms. "I don't need you to."

She marched away down a random path.

The path was very overgrown. Little Rude soon found herself in the middle of a thorny bush and realized she was very lost. She clambered up onto the top of a small bank, and started jumping up and down, to see if she could spot a way out.

A rabbit came scurrying out of a hole in the bank. "Good day!" the rabbit waved up at Little Rude. "My name is Mrs. Rabbit. Would you please stop jumping on top of my house?"

"I'll stop jumping if you tell me the way out of this stupid, ugly, thorny bush," said Little Rude.

"I can help you, but you need to say the magic word first," said Mrs. Rabbit.

Little Rude grinned as she did a big jump in the air. "Abracadabra!" she said.

Mrs. Rabbit had several children herself, and she always tried to teach them good manners. "That's not the word I meant," Mrs. Rabbit said, gently. "It starts with 'P.'"

"Presto!" Little Rude giggled, jumping up and down even more.

"You are a rude little girl and you can stay lost," said Mrs. Rabbit, going back into her burrow.

The thorns scratched Little Rude's hands and knees as she crawled through them.

It took a long time for Little Rude to crawl through the thorny patch, but finally she reached a riverbank. On the other side was Grandma's house!

A woodcutter stood on the riverbank with a small wooden boat.

"Good morning to you!" The woodcutter lifted his hat politely.

"I need a ride across the river," said Little Rude.

The woodcutter raised his eyebrows.

"Well, if you say the magic word, then you can get in line behind my other passengers."

Little Rude turned to see Mr. Wolf and Mrs. Rabbit and her family waiting patiently on the riverbank.

Little Rude never liked to be last in

anything, so she strolled over to the line and cut in at the very front.

Mr. Wolf growled.

"My boat is big enough for you all, but I won't take anyone who's rude," said the woodcutter, as he climbed into his boat and helped the animals on. He rowed them all across the river, leaving Little Rude behind.

"Hey, what about me?" Little Rude called out to the woodcutter. "Come back!"

But the woodcutter didn't take any notice of Little Rude. The boat glided across the river. Within minutes, he and the animals hopped off the boat onto the far riverbank. They skipped across the grass and went into Grandma's house.

"That's rude," Little Rude muttered to herself. "The woodcutter was taking the animals to see Grandma. He could have taken me too."

Without a boat, Little Rude had to wade across the cold river. She lifted the basket of cakes as high as she could, but they still got very wet. Her shoes filled up with water and her stockings were soaked through. She threw the ruined cakes in the river and watched them sink.

By the time Little Rude had crossed the river and arrived at Grandma's house, she was in a very bad mood.

"Let me in!" she shouted as she hammered on the door.

The woodcutter opened the door.

"Good afternoon," he said. "Would you like to come in?"

"Why are you answering the door? This isn't your house," said Little Rude, pushing past him.

"We're getting the house ready for a surprise birthday party for your Grandma," said the woodcutter.

"We sent her out for a lovely walk this morning," Mrs. Rabbit explained. "She'll be back soon."

"I've brought balloons," said Mr. Wolf. "Mr. Woodcutter has brought paperchains and the Rabbit family has brought food."

"Well, I brought cakes but they got ruined in the river," said Little Rude.

"Never mind!" Young Tessie Rabbit clapped her paws, "You can eat one of mine."

Little Rude walked over to the table and started to squash all of Tessie's cakes in her basket.

"Hey, leave some for the rest of us," Tessie cried.

"No, I won't," said Little Rude. "I'm going to eat them all by myself."

Tessie looked very sad.

"How rude," growled Mr. Wolf, "Tessie baked the cakes for everyone!"

The animals wished that Little Rude wasn't there. They worried that she was going to ruin the party with her rudeness.

"Would you like to help us with the decorations?" Mrs. Rabbit asked.

Little Rude flopped down in Grandma's armchair and put her dirty, wet feet up on the stool. "No, I'm tired from walking," she said.

"But we're all helping," said Tessie Rabbit.

"Make me," said Little Rude, grinning.

"Well, if you aren't going to help, please could you at least move out of the way?" asked the woodcutter. "I need to stand on the chair to finish hanging my paperchains."

"Oh, you'll just have to stretch, you lazy

thing," said Little Rude. "I'll sit where I like."

The woodcutter climbed onto a stool and leaned as far as he could over Little Rude's head. He reached and reached and ... fell! Off the stool he tumbled, down to the floor, along with all of the paperchains!

Mr. Woodcutter was really sad that his lovely decorations had been ruined.

"Never mind," Mrs. Rabbit comforted him. "Why don't we practise our song for Grandma instead?"

"It's her present from us. A special birthday song that we wrote," Tessie Rabbit explained to Little Rude.

"But you already brought cakes," said Little Rude.

"This is extra," said Tessie, smiling and clapping her paws.

Little Rude didn't want the animals to have a lovely extra present for Grandma when she didn't, so she waited until they started to sing, and then she blew a big raspberry.

They all stopped.

"You're ruining the song," said Mr. Wolf, sternly.

"No, I'm making it better," Little Rude replied, laughing to herself. "Your singing sounds like a bunch of cats fighting a bagpipe!"

She waited until they started again and then blew another raspberry.

Mr. Wolf had reached the end of his tether with Little Rude. He stomped over to her and roared, "WILL YOU STOP BEING SO RUDE?"

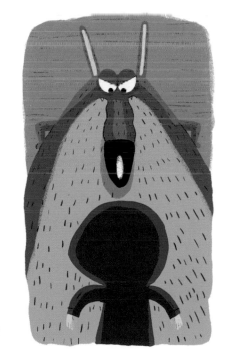

Little Rude was silent for a moment. Then, she poked out her tongue and blew one more big raspberry, right at Mr. Wolf.

"That's it!" bellowed Mr. Wolf. "If you don't stop right now, I will gobble you up!"

"Hah, you can't catch me! You're so slow, you'd lose a race against a sleepy snail." Little Rude put her thumbs in her ears and

waggled her fingers at Mr. Wolf. Then she
ran around the room, her red hood bouncing
behind her.

Mr. Wolf ran after Little Rude. He chased
her into a corner.

Little Rude wasn't scared. She turned and
laughed at him which made Mr. Wolf even
more angry.

"You know, I used to be known as The
Big Bad Wolf, before I learned some
manners," he growled.

"Hah, you're more
like a small, scared
squirrel with false
teeth. You'd never
eat me." Little Rude
laughed so much,
she didn't see Mr.
Wolf's big bad
mouth open right
over her head.

In the next moment, Mr. Wolf gobbled up Little Rude, her bad manners, and her red riding hood in one great, big gulp.

Mr. Wolf looked very guilty. "What have you done, Mr. Wolf?" the woodcutter said. "The rudeness has gone, but so has the little girl."

"Mr. Wolf has eaten Little Rude!" Mrs. Rabbit said. "What will Grandma say?"

"Grandma will be upset! Grandma will cry! On her birthday! Oh no!" the little rabbits cried.

At that moment, the front door opened, and Grandma walked in.

"Hello everyone! How lovely to see you all!" Grandma said with a big smile.

"Mr. Wolf, Mr. Woodcutter, Mrs. Rabbit!
Little rabbits, you are all grown up."
Grandma hugged each of her friends in turn.
She had no idea that something bad had just
happened. "What a lovely surprise! The
party can start as soon as my granddaughter,
Little Rude, arrives."

The party guests didn't know what to say.

The paperchains were all on the floor, the cakes were gone and Little Rude was stuck in Mr. Wolf's belly, but Mrs. Rabbit was trying to give Grandma a nice birthday. "Come on everyone," she called, "let's sing Grandma's birthday song. One, two, three–"

Mr. Wolf opened his mouth wide to sing: "BUUUURRRRRRRPP!"

"Mr. Wolf!" Grandma looked shocked. At that moment, Little Rude popped all the way out of Mr. Wolf's mouth!

"Granddaughter!" Grandma cried.

"Pardon me," said Mr. Wolf.

Little Rude looked up at him. She nearly said something rude like she normally did, but then she remembered the darkness inside his belly.

"Thank you, Grandma, you saved my life!" said Little Rude. "Mr. Wolf's belly was dark and it smelled like rotten old beans. I didn't want to stay there forever." Little Rude hugged Grandma tightly. "Thank you. Thank you. Thank you."

"How lovely to hear you say thank you," Grandma said. "I don't think I have ever heard you say it before."

"I've had a really horrible day," Little Rude said. "I got lost in the forest. I was scratched by brambles. Then I was soaked in the river and then I was gobbled up."

"Oh dear," said Grandma. "That does sound horrible."

"It was all my fault," said Little Rude. "I've always been rude to everyone, but I see now that if I had been nice, none of those things would have happened. Forgive me, everyone."

"What's the magic word?" the animals cried.

"Please!" Little Rude beamed.

Everybody cheered, and all was forgiven.

"And Grandma, thank you for my coat," said Little Rude. "It's beautiful and I love it."

"You are welcome, dear," Grandma said, smiling. "If you're not going to be rude anymore, we'll have to change your name to Little Red Riding Hood!"

"I have something to say, too," said Mr. Wolf. "I'm sorry for eating you. That part wasn't your fault at all."

Then Little Red and Mr. Wolf worked together to fix all the decorations.

The forest band arrived to play for the party and everybody danced together.

Little Red remembered all the magic words. She offered the cakes to everyone else before she took one, and when the party was over, she stayed to help clean up.

Everyone had a fantastic time, and Grandma said it was the best birthday she'd ever had.

"From now on, I'll always use good manners," Little Red promised herself as she walked home. Then she burped and giggled. "Well, most of the time!"